DUST BUNNY LIST

Dust Bunny List

Volume 2 Dark Maid
Sehseh

Sarah Elliot

Katrina Allcroft, Boo Lai

Sarah Elliot Author

CONTENTS

THANK YOUS

Sarah - A big thank you to all my family and friends, for all the times that you've been there for me.

Also big shout out to the creative team, Kat, Kurt and Boo because I would not be here without the three of you

Kat - Thanks to my fam, as well as Sophie and Kate for being a constant force of friendship and improvement in both art and mental health

~Boo and Kurt are happily floating in the mysts of shyness~

1

STICKERS

Sehseh took a moment to stare up at the darkening sky. She stretched as she made her way out of the door to the office block where Master Rhain resided during working hours, then tilted her head to the side, blinking up at the complicated swirls of grey, black, navy and orange with occasional smatters of red above her before a smile crossed her face. "Ah, twilight, my favourite time of day."

Rocking back and forth onto her toes and heels, Sehseh flicked her bunches over her shoulder and flipped open her PDA to check on her task list for the night. Rhain had said that there wasn't much to do, the dust bunnies were at a low ebb for the day. This was a silly notion, Sehseh thought, as there was always a crime being committed somewhere by someone, but she supposed that the higher levels were more concerned with the government audits that were going on. Master Rhain had been quite exhausted displaying all of his various charts, forms and records, and *they* were all fairly clean and legit. The Maid wondered what it would be like to have to hide everything illegally or present it as something else. It would be beyond exhausting, and in a way, it was probably a good thing that the dust bunnies didn't deal too much in their mischief after dealing with all of that.

Returning from her thoughts to her PDA, she scanned the list of jobs and household chores that she had to do, checking off those she had already done for the day and putting several to one side for tomorrow. She had just finished when a message bubble popped up, making her pause, blinking. Opening it, she took in the contents for five seconds before suddenly letting out a high-pitched squeal. Several workers looked up from their desks on the ground floor to stare in shock at the sight of a Battle Maid bouncing up and down like a hyperactive child.

"Yes! Three hundred stickers!" Sehseh yelled loudly, "Canine Pup is mine! Yippee!"

Her happy little bouncing dance was interrupted by her PDA flashing to life with a bright-sounding tune and Sehseh was quick to answer it, "Yes Master?"

"I can hear you from the twenty-fifth floor," Rhain chuckled gently, "I too got the notification. Well done."

"Can I go and get him now? Please?" Sehseh asked, hopping excitedly from foot to foot like it was Christmas morning and she was five years old. As her dress was sky blue with white frills, a full apron and white ribbons in her hair, Sehseh was the picture of sweetness and innocence. She even had matching dainty shoes and knee-high socks. "I promise that I'll deal with anything that I find on the way and be straight back."

Rhain chuckled lightly, "Let me just check that there's a store nearby that's still accepting the promotion and you can get to it in a reasonable amount of time."

Humming happily whilst she waited, still bouncing back and forth on her heels, Sehseh cast her eyes around the streets out of nothing more than habit and spotted what appeared to be an ice cream vendor not too far away. A smile crossed her face at the thought of being able to buy Master Rhain some ice cream on the way back from her little adventure but then she tilted her head to the side as she recognised the vendor. "Oh, Alvin got a new job?" she spoke aloud.

"Another one?" Rhain replied, sighing heavily, "Seriously? Why can't he just set himself up as a legit business already?"

Sehseh shrugged, "He wants to be free and able to do his work."

There was a snort of a reply, "Ha, more like he can't be bothered with doing the accounts properly and would rather run away from that responsibility. Ah, here we go. FPStore has the doll you're after with the stickers promotion and they're open till 6 pm tonight, so that gives you around an hour to get there."

Sehseh squealed again, "Yay! I'll go and get him right now... I may even have time to get rid of some more dust bunnies."

"Just remember to be back before seven thirty tonight," Rhain said, "You promised me Sehseh."

"I know, silly, that's why I'm going out now rather than later," Sehseh said, smiling brightly and then signed off from the call and headed straight towards the ice cream stall. She giggled at the sight of Alvin in a dull pair of trousers with a white jacket and a plastic pink pinny, serving ice cream to a pair of teenagers who looked just about ready to rob the neon green-haired seller. "Evening Alvin," Sehseh greeted brightly, stepping closer and shocking the two teenagers into paying and scurrying off as quickly as they could. "I thought you were working at-"

"Don't mention it," Alvin cut in with a sigh, "It's a job I don't want to ever go back to."

"Oh, and what about-"

Alvin shook his head, "Jerk wasn't worth the time of day. Thought that BJs were free of charge and didn't have to repay the favour."

Sehseh blinked and shook her head, "Aww, that's a shame. Found anyone new yet?"

"Maybe I should stay single for a bit," Alvin mused half-heartedly, "It seems the best way."

"Oh, I don't think it would do you any good at all sweet-heart," a deep rumbling voice cut across and the pair turned to see a rather charming man in a slick suit, with black hair pulled back and a smirk that spoke of mischief and danger in abundance. "Someone as dashing as you should be hanging off the right arm of the most perfect man."

About to shoot off a snarky reply, the Maid instead sighed. Sehseh recognised the man as a corporate pig whom Rhain occasionally had to deal with and fend off some rather lewd advances from, despite making it clear that he wasn't interested in the slightest. Alvin was leaning forward with a challenging look in his eyes, clearly interested and already planning nasty things that he could do with this one. Shaking her head, Sehseh waved it off and started down the road. "Call me when you want to be rid of this stinky man, Alvin."

Though she paused and turned back around, "Oh and Master Rhain says to stay out tonight if you can...but I suppose you've got your own date sorted now, eh?"

There was no response from Alvin and Sehseh once again rolled her eyes but skipped merrily along as she set off towards the FPStore with the sole intent of obtaining her Canine Pup plushie. She had been saving up for it for ages and she couldn't wait to have it in her possession. Accessing her internal map of the city, Sehseh estimated that it would take roughly twenty minutes for her to get to the shop, obtain the plush and then return, so she had plenty of time and wouldn't have to worry too much about delays, even with the rush hour traffic that was spilling into the streets from all of the high-raised buildings as the sun continued to dip down below the horizon.

Humming brightly, Sehseh continued along and she had to remind herself not to squeal constantly in anticipation of what she was finally about to achieve. Nothing seemed out of the ordinary until her thoughts were suddenly interrupted by a startled cry of a woman. She turned towards the sound and saw a man in dark red clothes and a mask marked with a black circle and a white dot in the middle. He was holding onto a woman whilst a second man was standing in front of her, holding up a very sharp-looking knife. The second man looked almost identical to the first, bar he had a golden dot inside the white dot, which Sehseh knew marked him as being one of the leaders.

An annoyed groan left Sehseh's lips as she put her hands on her hips. "I thought I had already dealt with enough of you guys to give you a hint or two."

The White Dot Gang had been causing trouble around the neighbourhood for many years and Sehseh had plenty of dealings with them. She had thought that going to their hideout and virtually wiping them all out had been enough, but clearly, there were more of the extremely naughty dust bunnies that she would have to deal with once again.

Gold-Dot snarled inside his mask, leaning closer to the woman who was shivering in the hold of one of his lackeys. "Right, ducky, last chance. Hand over your money and credit cards and then we'll leave you be. Not that hard is it?"

Lackey took a too-loud sniff at the woman's neck, seeming to savour it for just a moment. "Hmm, pretty little bitch smells nice. Maybe we can have some fun with this one eh Gold-Dot?"

A slap was sharply delivered to the side of his head. "Shut up you moron. This one ain't pretty enough for that. Now come on, sweetie pie, let's be having what we asked for and it won't get any nastier than it has."

Gold-Dot grabbed the woman's handbag, snapping the handle clean away from her body, and flipped it open. He expected to find her purse and credentials inside but was instead met by a mirror which showed only the reflection of a young-looking girl with dark brown hair, deep blue eyes that were lined with red eyeshadow and an annoyed expression upon her face.

He spun around fast in terror. "Not you again!"

Sehseh glared at him. "Yes, me again."

"But...but you're not..." Gold-Dot started, then glanced down at the bag in his hand, "Oh this! No, we were returning this to her. We found it you see!"

"Boss?" Lackey asked, sounding very unsure.

Sehseh narrowed her eyes. "Do you think I'm that dumb?"

"I'm hoping so," Gold-Dot said, and realised a second later that he had said the wrong thing. Sehseh's foot landed smartly in his jaw as she roundhouse kicked him straight to the ground, two teeth flying out of him as his head hit the pavement.

"Dumb bitch!" Lackey yelled, shoving the woman who would have been his victim away to point a gun in the direction of the Maid. "Suck on lead!"

Checking the List Off

2

MUGGING BUNNY GOES DOWN

The smoke from the bullet hadn't even had time to finish fanning out before Sehseh was charging straight into Lackey. Her fist connected with his gut, followed by her knee swiftly to his face, producing a very unhealthy-sounding cracking noise. Lackey spat blood onto the floor and doubled over onto the pavement, groaning heavily and seeming unable to breathe. Sehseh was quick to stamp on his hand as it shakily attempted to go for the gun again, more bones breaking from the pressure alone.

Flicking her head back over her shoulder, her eyes bored straight into Gold-Dot, standing as still as a statue right where she had left him. She raised an eyebrow towards the man, who thought for a moment, then pulled open his jacket and rummaged through the pockets. From within, he produced two ladies' purses, a PDA with a cute dog phone cover and a necklace which was probably a piece of costume jewellery but looked pretty. Turning to the woman who had been technically his victim, the tall man was shaking as he held out the items towards her.

The woman blinked in confusion and she glanced towards the items, then towards Sehseh, then back at Gold-Dot, then down at Lackey gasping on the ground. Slowly. she brought her eyes back up to Sehseh, staring at the girl as if she had never seen anything like her before.

(This was probably very true. Whilst Maids and Butlers were commonplace amongst the rich clientele, the workers typically only saw them either at posh events, in the medical centres where they could sometimes afford the treatment or were granted special access or more typically when they were on the wrong end of pissing someone off.)

"Please," Gold-Dot managed to stammer out without dropping too many letters to his words, "She won't let him go until you take your stuff back. I'm very sorry, I'll make sure that no one in our gang ever targets you again...please, he's going to bleed out at this rate and I really can't afford to lose him right now."

Blinking again, the woman reached forward and took back her PDA and purse, shaking her head towards the necklace. Gold-Dot shoved it back into his pocket, but a very firm 'Ahem' made him take it out and drop it to the ground. Two long seconds passed before Gold-Dot rushed forward to grab hold of Lackey, hauling him upright and running both of them in the opposite direction away from the crazy Maid.

Sehseh sighed and shook her head, "Oh honestly, I wonder how many more times I'll have to deal with those silly bunnies."

"Erm, thank you," the woman said softly, blinking towards the Maid. "Erm, are you with the defence forces?"

Letting out a long giggle at that thought, Sehseh shook her head and pirouetted around, "Nope! Those guys are a load of phoney anyway."

"Oh," the lady went, blinking, "Then why?"

"Got to earn my stickers for the Space Buddies Plushies somehow," Sehseh happily exclaimed, bouncing up onto the balls of her feet once again. "Oh, that reminds me, I need to get to the shop before it closes. Nice to have helped you, Mrs Worker, don't let any nasty bunnies take your things again." Bending down, she scooped up the stolen loot, carefully put it into her white bunny backpack and then went skipping down the street as if nothing were out of the ordinary. She had lost a little bit of time, but it was nothing that she could not catch up with. Even with a stop-off at the 'Lost and Found' she would still have plenty of time. Though she did remember to put tracer marks on the items this time to ensure that they were indeed going back to the correct people and not being used for other purposes.

Humming brightly as she made her way along the rough-hewed pavement, Sehseh came to an abrupt stop once again when she heard the screeching of car tyres. Slowly the Maid turned, a frown forming on her face. This was a pedestrianised area and there were not supposed to be any kind of vehicles there, not even those little road sweepers that went around (though secretly Sehseh had always thought that they'd be rather fun to drive around).

She watched in amazement as a red car (though it was impossible to tell from this distance whether that had been the original colour or it had gone that rusty) spun in a haphazard circle before charging directly into the front of one of the stores. Glass smashed outwards, scattering across the pavement, the alarm bell ringing almost pointlessly. The doors opened and five female figures stepped out, swinging either bats or some kind of makeshift weapons.

Each one was dressed in a virtually identical outfit, a black form-fitting top with long sleeves, a tutu-style skirt, striped black and white socks and heavy combat boots. Each one wore a stylised face mask in their own unique colour with matching bunny ears. Sehseh recognised the colours easily. Red for Shazza, yellow for ZoomZoom, pink for Titi, purple for Mellow and green for Jena. The girls of the P.A.B. group. Sehseh could have yelled in frustration but managed to stay quiet, especially when she realised that the smug driver wore a black and baby blue outfit matching the others.

Sehseh blinked, checked her internal clock and ran through her database on previous encounters with the P.A.B. Group to approximate how long it would take her to deal with them. She estimated about fifteen minutes if they were up for a real fight, which they probably were. They were looting a particularly high-end fashion store that was way out of their usual price range, so it was probably that someone had hired them to steal the latest collection. Sehseh sighed long and hard. "Well,

I'll still have fifteen minutes clear, best get these little bunnies cleared out of the way."

She skipped forward and peered into the gloom that was the remains of the shop, tilting herself carefully so that there was some cover should ZoomZoom be on the watch, and prepared to throw her knives. Zoomzoom was always loaded with hundreds of throwing knives, and combined with her black-market robotic eyes, hitting the exact weak spot was almost impossible to miss. Sehseh had personally dealt with this gang on three separate occasions and the only reason she hadn't eliminated them was due to them having information. It was dangerous information that came with a too-high price, but it was just the sort of thing that would be needed to eventually take out the ultimate Dust Bunny himself.

Plus, unlike most of the gangs around Neocastle, these girls were at least working towards a sort of respectable goal. They stole from high-end retail stores; sold the goods they got to the highest bidder and then took the money back to the orphanage where they had grown up. There they would pay any outstanding bills, play with the kids and help out before heading back onto the streets to cause more mayhem and mischief. They weren't quite the respectable outlaws of the day, as they were extremely selfish and didn't share the money with anyone else, but there was at least a point to what they were doing.

Hearing a squeak of surprise, Sehseh turned her line of vision away from the wrecked store and blinked towards the girl sitting behind the driver's wheel. Her baby blue face mask and pointed ears easily identified her as Totz, the youngest member of the gang, who was generally the most protected and least likely to cause trouble unless needed. Her eyes were large with a mixture of recognition and fright as she stared towards Sehseh. The Maid raised her eyebrow at Totz. "Why is it that you girls can't just get an ordinary job or save up enough money to run a café or something?" Sehseh asked, politely, as she knew it was a bad idea to try and threaten her.

Another squeak was her response and Totz's hand hit the car's horn, blaring out a warning sound that drove straight through Sehseh's audio. Startled by the sound, she staggered backwards and crouched down with her hands over her ears. Suddenly business alarms were blaring all around them, glass cracking across the adjoining shops and then a long white noise whistle.

It was only experience that made the Maid stand upright and turn, a fraction too late, to block an attack from a blur of green which was quickly followed by a barrelling roll move from a small, compact, pink-coloured mask that had both Maid and Titi sprawled on the floor in a matter of seconds. Hitting her head off the pavement, Sehseh winced and pushed upwards with all her might. Titi rolled backwards with a natural grace and was poised in the pounce position with heavy, angry eyes.

Sehseh sighed and rubbed at her head for a second, trying to shake off a sudden wave of nausea. She turned and glared towards the crouched girl. "That was so mean, Titi, I was only asking Totz a question."

"Shit!" Titi hissed, turning to glare at the green-masked Jena. "I thought you said that she would be distracted tonight!"

"From all intel she was!" Jena argued back, clearly trying not to panic but doing so anyway.

The two girls started bickering and Sehseh groaned as she stood up, still rubbing the side of her head. She shook herself to clear the slightly odd glitch that was suddenly filtering into her vision. Her internal medical system was trying to warn her about something, but the algorithms were completely off so the data would be best described as gobbledegook. Sehseh blinked, ignoring it, and then turned with her hands on her hips to face the red-masked girl nearby.

"We made a deal, Shazza," she stated firmly, "Are you going back on it?

P.A.B Girls on their raid

3

P.A.B

Shazza was fairly tall, with a strong build, a distinctive red face mask and red ears. She was dressed to match the other girls, but what made her stand out more than anything else was the solid metal plate spanning from the base of her neck down to just above her belly button. It was a dull metal colour, with small crisscrosses of rust creeping around the edges, caused by natural blood flow produced by the body. A few clear access panels showed through, though they were grimy and ill-kept with a dull orange glow coming from them. The tell-tale signs of a back street body job. Sehseh tried not to think about the amount of pain that Shazza would be in with such shoddy work. Death would have probably been the saner option, but for someone like Shazza, there was no other choice. If there was any chance at survival, the stupid fool would have taken it, no matter the consequences. As long as she could keep the orphanage going, the leader of P.A.B. would do so.

Shazza shook her head, "No. We're not going back on our deal."

"I rather think you are," Sehseh said, never taking her eyes off Shazza, "Especially considering ZoomZoom and Mellow are moving to ideal attack positions on either side of me."

The leader didn't even bat an eyelid at being caught out so easily. "We're only breaking the looting part; we're not going to hurt anyone."

"Who-" Sehseh paused, flicked a warning finger towards Totz, waggling it back and forward a couple of times to make sure that the youngest put down the baseball bat that she had been slowly raising before turning her attention fully back to Shazza. "Who hired you?"

A shake of the head was her reply, "You know I can't say that."

Sehseh tilted her head to the side, "Why?"

"Because that's not how the game works, Sehseh, and you know it," Shazza said, sighing as she shook her head. "Are you going to deal with us now or give us a head start?"

"You're not going to back down?" Sehseh sounded genuinely upset, "But you always back down."

"Not tonight," Shazza shrugged, "There's nothing I can do. We need this job."

Sehseh narrowed her eyes, "Don't tell me you went back to him."

Before a syllable of a reply could even form on the red leader's lips, Sehseh found herself being knocked to the floor by a punch to the back of her head. She landed on the pavement on her hands and knees, only to be kicked firmly in her stomach which forced her into the side of the car. Mellow was on her immediately, grabbing her head to smash it against the metal and something squished.

A jolt shot through Sehseh, painful and as clear as a bell. Her vision blacked out and when it returned everything was in a stark black and white. She blinked, trying to clear her vision but was instead met with a fist to the face repeatedly. Vaguely she could hear someone yelling in the background but couldn't focus on the words and the next thing she knew or understood, Sehseh found herself lying on her back in the middle of Northumberland Street with Mellow holding her down whilst ZoomZoom hovered dangerously close with a knife.

"Don't worry Sehseh, this will just a be minor little prick and then you'll pass out for a bit." The eye smile was entirely inappropriate for this situation but Sehseh supposed it could have been worse. "Sorry that it's got to be like this but..."

The tip of the knife penetrated just under her left ear and a second jolt shot through Sehseh's body so harshly that she physically bucked upwards and caused ZoomZoom to topple to the side with a yelp. Colour bled into the black-and-white world that Sehseh had been staring at, caused by the blood which leaked down as she saw hundreds of images in too quick succession to be able to follow them. A little girl in a wheelchair, medication, reports, strange men. Alvin being fascinated with her, a computer programmer, a little girl on a swing, too many cars, a van, darkness and a cage. Pain, needles, stitches, a friendly hand in the dark, a promise spoken and forgotten, bloody knife, gunshot, Mr Wirth standing over her saying something but the words garbled, error messages, primary directive, must protect Little Miss!

A scream tore from her throat and Sehseh launched herself upright, dragging Mellow along with her before slamming the girl to the ground and twisting her arm so much that it broke. ZoomZoom stabbed forward with her knife, catching the Maid in her shoulder causing another howl of pain before the yellow-clad girl was suddenly thrown across the opposite side of the street where she collided with a bench and rag-dolled down to the floor. Sehseh was up on her feet in the next second, disorientated and searching around desperately for something.

A blur of purple caused her to spin out of the way just in time to avoid a kick that was sent her way and she deflected a barrel roll from Titi causing her to crash into Jenna. The pair were quick to respond, tag-teaming into a swift in-and-out routine of punches, kicks, headbutts and nails in a recurring but unpredictable pattern as they moved back and forth so quickly it was impossible to stop one without getting caught by the other. Sehseh interrupted the pattern by simply ducking when they both happened to do a high kick at the same time, their boots clashing together. Sehseh's hands shot up and with speed unlike anything else, she undid the laces and retied them together in a complicated knot before throwing their now-joined feet straight back over her shoulder. Both Titi and Jenna crashed to the floor, and Sehseh swiftly turned and smacked both of their heads together with a heavy-sounding 'thunk'. She repeated the process three more times until neither girl responded and then let them slump down to the ground.

She stood up, her balance back, and Shazza faced her standing her ground. Whether she had that much bravado or she was just too scared to do anything, it didn't matter. The Maid grabbed the knife in her shoulder, pulled it out with slow and precise movements and then charged straight towards the remaining threat.

"Noooo!" a young voice squealed. "Stop! Please! Don't hurt..."

"Totz!"

Sehseh suddenly found herself holding onto the youngest of the P.A.B members, whose body was stiff and unresponsive. Her large, adorable eyes were even wider now and laced with tears that began to trickle down her face. The knife blade was cold inside her stomach and a whimper left Totz's lips. "Please.... don't hurt...my big sister..." Totz stammered out, "She's the only family I got left."

Shazza grabbed the girl, pulling her back from Sehseh to lay her down and apply pressure to the wound, "Totz! You fucking idiot! Why did you do that?"

Totz smiled, "Because... you would... for me..." a pained cry left her lips, "Hurts!"

"Oh no! Totz, what happened?" Sehseh's voice suddenly cut in and Shazza looked up. There was Sehseh, kneeling next to them with too-bright glimmering eyes, the murderous expression suddenly gone from her face. Even though there was blood coming out of Sehseh's shoulder, she only seemed worried about the younger girl. "You've got a stab wound to your lower stomach and it appears to have glanced your hip bone, but I've already called the ambulance and they'll be here shortly."

The girl in red blinked. "What the hell?"

Sehseh turned her eyes up towards Shazza. "What happened here, Shazza?"

"What happened?" Shazza asked, sounding unbelieving, "You just went fucking ape-shit and took out virtually all my girls! That's what happened you fucking shit!"

Sehseh blinked and looked around, "Oh? I did this?"

"Yes, you..." Shazza turned her attention back to the crying Totz. "What the fuck? I get what you have to do but we have a deal..."

"I know... hmm, I think I need to speak to Alvin about this," Sehseh replied, turning her attention back to Totz and then grabbing at the bottom of her skirt and ripping off two full circles of material. With precision like nothing Shazza had ever seen before, the Maid had the wound wrapped tightly in a few seconds. "It's best to keep the pressure applied here," she guided Shazza's hand to an extra knot and made her squeeze it, "It won't completely stop the blood flow, but it'll slow it down and the medical assistants will be able to sort out the flow much easier this way."

Shazza stared, "You really don't know what you did, do you?"

"Don't worry about the bills," Sehseh continued, a little smile making its way to her face, "Master Rhain says he will cover it and if you give me a name... I'll deal with them."

Shazza just stared. "Why?"

A sad smile crossed Sehseh's face. "How long are you expected to live?"

"Long enough," Shazza replied, gulping as she pulled Totz closer. "Will she live?"

Sehseh nodded. "She will. Oh, look the paramedics are here. Name?"

Shazza looked over at the androids rushing towards them and then turned. "Mrs Vidyut. The arranged one."

Standing up, Sehseh stepped to the side to allow the medical personnel to get access to Totz and the others before quietly slipping away unnoticed. Quickly, she sent off messages to Rhain, Alvin and Sunny, thinking it best to give the info specialist a heads-up about some serious research that was coming her way before she blew a gasket at everyone. Another sticker popped up on her screen and Sehseh blinked, "Oh! Canine Pup! How long left...oh ten minutes! Easy! Let's go!"

Rushing off, Sehseh headed towards the shop which had her prize plushie waiting in the window and she grinned happily at being able to see the toy standing proud with his arms open wide as if waiting for a cuddle. Sehseh pressed her nose up against the glass, her eyes all aglow like a little child as she was so close to it that she could practically feel the fuzzy fur.

A scream ripped through the otherwise silent night and Sehseh turned just in time to see a little girl with brown hair and an adorable pink pinafore dress being dragged into a van. Her father was screaming blue murder from a bloody puddle nearby and a familiar feeling of fear, loathing and anger crossed Sehseh's heart.

"Sorry, Canine Pup, but it's time to take out some very naughty bunnies," she said out loud, pressing a button in her wrist to call her sweeping brush to her side. "No one steals a child on my watch!"

Dust Bunny Daycare

4

TYNE BRIDGE TAKE OUT

"Do me a favour and shut that fucking brat up!"

The van driver yelled at his passengers, swerving around the corner just a little too fast. He had to weave around a bollard at the end of the street, designed to stop drivers like him from getting into the main pedestrianised areas. There was a very harsh scraping sound, but no one was bothered. The van was already pretty beaten up before the Snappers took it, and as long as it had working wheels and was able to be driven, then the outward appearance didn't matter. Once the order was completed, the van would be dumped into the Tyne anyway, where the age-old soup of water would swallow it up without a complaint.

The thought occurred that if anyone was ever brave enough, the number of unsolved crimes that could be sorted out from dredging up the Tyne would be astronomical in proportions, but the water wasn't known to be that willing, especially now that it had formed some odd awareness. A biological weapon had been fired by the enemy during the fourth world war

26

had completely missed its intended target, ending up in the River Tyne. No one knew exactly if the bomb had cracked and leaked, or if the outer casing had dissolved, but there was a certain quality in the water that made it very self-aware. It didn't seem to do much with this ability, other than drowning those who were too curious for their own good or throwing jumpers back out of it. Very occasionally, it would erupt into a beautiful display of fountains and colours that stank to high heaven and caused the quayside areas to be shut down for a month whilst the clean-up crews got to work, whilst avoiding any more 'playful' sprays that came from the river.

But the driver, a pock-faced man called Ben, had no intention of going anywhere near the Tyne tonight, as the back roads were more than sufficient for an escape. The Enforcers wouldn't react, of course. The cameras in the area were all on a twenty-minute delay, and by the time the Enforcers saw the crime being committed, the van would be long gone.

One of the gang members turned to the captured girl who was screaming the place down, and pressed a chloroform-covered handkerchief over her mouth and nose. The girl hiccupped a few times as the drug quickly took effect and she slumped down to the floor of the van.

One of the other gang members snarled at him. "Goddamn it, Clive! Why didn't you just do that in the first place?"

"You didn't let me have any, Blink," Clive snarled back, now trying to light a cigarette but failing, "Said after the last time…"

"Oh, shut up," Blink snapped, setting the girl down next to the others. "At least that's the last one. Could have done without the father screaming though. The fucking useless man will probably be-"

The van suddenly lurched to the side, and Blink's head bounced against the interior wall. "What the fuck, Ben?!"

"Shit! Bugger it all to hell!" Ben yelled, slamming the brakes on and wheeling the van around to the other side, causing the two men in the back to tumble into the opposite wall.

"What the fuck are you doing, you fuck nugget?!" Blink screamed, "You're sending us the wrong-"

Once again, Blink was forced to momentarily shut up as they were thrown around again, this time from an impact. "What the fuck has gotten you so fucked up?"

Ben did not reply, instead pulling another sharp turn and slamming a button marked 'Nitro Boost', followed by a series of expletives that were barely full words.
"Ben!" Blink yelled again as the van stalled and screeched to a standstill. He scrambled forward to slap the much taller guy around the back of his head, who was desperately trying to restart the van. "You better have a fucking good excuse..."

There came a 'ping' sound of metal being pierced, and Blink spun round to find a long wooden stick coming through the left-hand side of the van. The end of the stick was buried deep into Clive's neck, who was staring down at it in shock. The next second, the stick left the way it entered, jerking out of Clive's throat and through the side of the van like it was nothing more than butter, leaving an opening that was only a couple of inches thick. As Clive dropped to the floor with a thud, a pair of dark blue eyes lined with red eyeshadow appeared through the hole.

"Peek-a-Boo!" Sehseh chirruped.

"Shit! Drive!" Blink yelled and Ben slammed his foot on the accelerator as hard as he could. The engine roared into life, lurching dangerously forward as if it had been caught on something before pulling free and rushing off.

Blink climbed into the passenger seat next to Ben, ripping open the glove box and pulling out a gun which practically fell to pieces in his hands.

"What the fuck is this cheap ass shit-" he began to say to himself, before spotting a taser gun behind where he'd found the pistol. He made a grab for it and started fumbling with the plastic covering before glancing out of the window. Big mistake.

"This is the A167? You're going to take us to the bridge!"

"I've got no other choice," Ben said, slamming down the gears to get more traction even though the engine was screeching in protest. "She'd be fucking insane trying to follow us across that thing."

Blink glanced at the wing mirror, spotting a sweeping brush sticking out of the side of the van in a fresh hole that must've been made as the van set off. He turned to look back at the now-dead body of Clive and winced. "Death by broom. What a way to go."

"She's not following us, is she?" Ben asked, manoeuvring around a burnt-out wreck as he took the underpass.

Blink looked at the wing mirror again, then carefully poked his head out of the window, taking a long look around before pulling himself back in, "Can't see the bitch."

"Good. We'll take the long way around," Ben replied, swapping gears down again. For the briefest of moments, he thought that he saw a streak of baby blue go along the pedestrian pavement and then up onto the familiar green arch of the Tyne Bridge. He shook his head. Nothing more than a trick from the river. "I mean, it'll be shitty, but after that..."

Blink nodded. "Yeah, plus we can get rid of Clive." There was no grief in his voice. "Bastard will be a liability no matter... what..."

Blink's voice trailed off, words failing him, and he simply stared, completely mystified by what he was seeing. Directly in front of the van was Sehseh. He saw a pair of creamy white legs and pink knickers first, then a blue dress, a white pinafore apron, adorable bunches and finally Sehseh's face, with an expression set to kill. She had jumped down in front of them from what could have only been the topmost bar of the Tyne Bridge, and just before the van caught up with her, she landed, stood up and held her hand out in a stop motion.

The sound of the collision amplified in the stillness of the growing darkness as the van crashed into the Maid and continued straight over her before toppling to the side and rolling over three times. It came to a stop with a tired-sounding huff and a scraping of metal on tarmac. For a few long moments, everything was still. Then the van's back doors were ripped cleanly off their hinges. Blink groaned from where he had landed, flung into the back of the van, and looked up to see the Maid who had followed them. A whimper of fear escaped from him.

Sehseh was standing, her dress in tatters, her hair a mess, more blood splattered over her form than should have been allowed for a living being and a very angry expression on her face. "You should have stopped," she commented dryly, "You could have hurt the children."

Blink paused and glanced at the three little girls they had captured that evening, still unconscious and strapped into the van's back seats. He turned back to the Maid. In a split second, he made his decision, flinging himself upright with a growl on his lips as he charged forward. His fist connected with her face, followed swiftly by his knee to her stomach and he then pushed her back before slamming his taser into her arm. "Take this, you bitch!"

He pressed the button on the device and felt the vibration as hundreds of volts of electricity shot down the connecting wires and into the girl's arm. There was a smell of burning plastic and sparks flew out of the contact point but instead of the screams of terror he expected, Blink found himself hearing a giggle in reply. "Stop that!" Sehseh laughed, her fingers grabbing onto the wires, "That tickles!"

With her movement completely unimpeded, Sehseh pulled the taser away from her skin and headbutted the dumbfounded man in one smooth motion, sending him to the floor. She kicked him firmly in the balls before climbing onto him, straddling his body with her own. The wind had been knocked out of Blink, and he coughed harshly as he scrabbled at her.

"Oh no, naughty bunny," Sehseh tutted. "You're going to stay right here. The Enforcers want to talk to you about stealing these children. If you keep on squirming, I'll have to cut off your airflow to-"

Sehseh stopped herself as Blink's head suddenly exploded in a shower of blood and brains. She pulled back in shock before raising her head very slowly. Standing roughly two hundred feet away at the opposite end of the bridge was a young girl, no older than sixteen.

The unknown girl wore a white shirt, with a blue fitted waistcoat over a knee-length skirt that was green-chequered with occasional blue lines over it. Black tights and a dark blue blazer embellished with a gold cat in a circle finished off the look. Her long blond hair was held in a high ponytail, tied up with a red bow, and the long lengths swept down almost reaching her knees. Her face was soft, young, and innocent, but Sehseh recognised the instinctive green eyes of a killer. She also recognised an air-sound weapon when she saw one, as she noted the toy plastic gun in the girl's hands.

The girl approached Sehseh and the body of Blink, smirking and raising an eyebrow.

She looked down at Sehseh, weapon raised, and spoke. "Oh well... I guess I can't kill you now, can I Seraphina? That would kill the game just a little too early." She giggled, "Though I am annoyed that you've stolen three from me."

Sehseh stared back in confusion towards the schoolgirl assassin standing in front of her, not knowing how to even react.

The girl blinked, taken aback, and the next time she spoke there was concern in her voice. "Wait. You do know me, don't you, Seraphina?"

Sehseh narrowed her eyes. "No. Should I?"

The girl lowered her weapon and took a step back, visibly shocked. "Daddy wasn't lying?"

"What are you on about?" Sehseh asked, getting to her feet and calling a dagger to her hand. A schoolgirl assassin was never a good start to a situation. A warning blip appeared on her iris as she continued to look at the girl, but she chose to ignore it for now. "Who are you?"

"How can you say that?!" The girl screamed at her, looking extremely upset. "You were made for me! You were the one who was supposed to protect me! You died for me, Seraphina! You gave up everything for me!"

Sehseh blinked, stepping forward, her head tilted in a mix of curiosity and confusion. "That is not my name."

"Fuck," the girl cursed, "He really did it, didn't he? He erased you! He made you someone else so he wouldn't have to feel guilty about what he had done."

Sehseh paused and turned away as she heard the sounds of sirens approaching the scene. The Enforcers were arriving ahead of schedule. Turning back, Sehseh found herself looking at an empty space where the girl had been. She glanced around and spotted a small pin on the ground depicting a golden cat. She knelt to pick it up and looked at it, frowning for just a second.

"Little..." she blinked again, "Miss?"

The Schoolgirl Assassin

5

CANINE PUP

"How come even when you go out to get a toy, you end up getting yourself in so much trouble, hmm?" Rhain asked as he appeared in the back of the service van, looking as calm as ever. Inside, he was already panicking over the state that his Maid was in. Even if he hadn't already been aware that she'd just been run over by a car, it would have been safe to assume as much from her overall look.

Sehseh raised her head and smiled brightly, waving at Rhain as if nothing were wrong in the slightest.

"Hello Master Rhain! You didn't need to come all the way out here to collect little old me. I could have gotten home just fine once these nice fixers are finished with me."

Rhain sighed, "Oh I know that, but there was a certain other fusspot who insisted we came along."

"Sod off, you big old-fashioned twerp!" Alvin came barging in, looking as though he had just run the mile from the High Street to the Bridge, "I have every right to be a fusspot!" He smacked Rhain firmly on the arm with a glare before roughly shoving him to one side and throwing himself at Sehseh with an overly dramatic wail. "Oh, my precious little unit! Look what those mean monsters have done to you! Are your systems okay? Are there any major breaks? Do I need to call Sunny and get some scans done on you?" He took a moment to actually breathe and then wailed as he realised the state Sehseh was in, "And what happened to your dress?! It should have easily survived a car accident!"

"It was actually a van," Sehseh giggled, smiling at his concern. "It went straight over the top of me."

Alvin paused and looked at her. "What?"

"The van, it went over the top of me," Sehseh repeated, then got distracted by a bleep on her phone.

Alvin turned to look at Rhain in complete disbelief. The older man nodded as he continued to straighten out his suit. "It smashed into her after she had landed in front of it from the top of the bridge."

"Their breaks were no good," Sehseh chimed in. "I was making the stop signs and they didn't respond accordingly."

Alvin opened his mouth to respond, then took a deep breath and closed it again, lowering his arms. He continued to take deep breaths as he formed his next words, trying to keep himself just a little more on the calm and rational side of things. "Sehseh, why on Earth did you drop down from the top of the bridge into a speeding van?"

"Because of them," the Maid replied, smiling as she waved towards something outside. Alvin and Rhain turned, finding an Enforcement Office being accompanied by a Nanny Maid who was comforting three little girls who were all crying. Each one had blond hair, blue eyes and an adorable expression even through the tears.

Alvin shuddered and turned back towards Sehseh, easily able to guess why those three had been chosen out of the hundreds that roamed the streets. He sighed again. "How did you find out about them?"

"Saw them taking one, decided to intervene," Sehseh replied, now checking something on her PDA to hide a deadly serious look that came over her face. "There's only one place that these bunnies could have been taking them and I'm not going to allow any other little girls to…"

Rhain gently patted Sehseh on the top of her head. "We know. You did good."

"What about the girls?" Alvin asked, looking back towards the trio.

"Their families are being located," Rhain replied. "By the looks of things, they've all got one."

"Thank fuck for that," Alvin replied. "We're already almost at capacity at…"

"Aww no!" Sehseh suddenly exclaimed, pouting dramatically.

Both boys turned to look at her, "What's wrong?"

"Canine Pup's gone!" Sehseh replied, looking miserable. "I checked the store listing 'cause I knew it would be closed by now but someone else got him just before they closed. It'll be months before they get another one in."

"Aww, that's a shame," Rhain replied, petting Sehseh again, "Don't worry. You'll get your chance to have one. Plus, you'll be close to getting Panther Kit by that point as well."

Sehseh still pouted dramatically and let out a defeated sigh. "But I was going to get him today."

"Don't worry, why don't we get you home and you can have a marathon of the movies, okay?" Rhain said, making a sign towards Alvin to shut up when the other seemed to want to protest about the action.

Gently Sehseh nodded and stood up, following Rhain out of the service van and into the awaiting four-by-four with its black glitter bodywork. Rhain ensured that Sehseh was secured in the front seat, whilst Alvin huffed himself into the back. He moaned about being there but was already beginning to set up one of his numerous laptops to start work on a new outfit for Sehseh and get some basic diagnostics going on her systems. Neither of the front passengers thought to ask him about what had happened to his new potential date for the night, and it was probably for the best that they hadn't.

They were five minutes into the drive when Sehseh blinked and pulled the small gold pin out of her pocket. She looked at it with curious eyes. Rhain glanced at her, "What's that?"

"Something a girl left behind," Sehseh replied, flipping it around in her fingers a couple of times, "She called me a strange name and seemed upset that I did not recognise her. But I don't know why."

Alvin snatched the pin out of her fingertips and stared at it. "What did the girl do?"

"Killed the bunny who survived the crash," Sehseh replied, "Using just a plastic gun. She knew what she was doing. Called me a strange name."

"What name?" Rhain asked, sounding very serious all of a sudden.

For a brief moment, the name was on the tip of the Maid's tongue, but then she suddenly stopped and looked out the window. It had begun to rain and idly her eyes followed the patterns of the droplets as they went down the window. Something stirred within her, a feeling that she shouldn't say anything else. That it would be a bad idea to say anything, because then the game would be up.

"Sehseh," Rhain said, his voice extremely serious now.

"Why the hell is Sunny bitching at me?" Alvin cut in, "What did you ask her to look into? Seriously, give me some warning before you do that."

"I did!" Sehseh replied, turning to look at Alvin, "I sent you a message first and then sent one to Sunny."

The argument continued all the way back to the Mansion, and it was only the appearance of Alvin's new apparent boyfriend that ended it. Instead, it was only to start shouting at the man and both Master and Maid exchanged a knowing glance before heading straight inside.

"Does Master want tea?" Sehseh asked as soon as they entered, heading in the direction of the kitchen only to be pulled back by Rhain.

"No, Master wants Sehseh to go to her room, rest and watch Space Buddies Movies for the rest of the night," Rhain stated, staring directly at her. "You've done more than you needed tonight so you need to rest."

Sehseh pouted. "But Master is hungry and Mister Fox...."

"Master will order take-out for us all and Mister Fox will come and watch those terrible movies with you as long as you go to your room right now and rest, Sehseh," Rhain stated again. "I'm not going to take no for an answer and you're not sneaking out to deal with any more dust puppies tonight."

A giggle came his way. "Bunnies, Master Rhain, it's naughty dust bunnies."

"Whatever. Bedroom, now," Rhain insisted, giving the girl a push, which caused her to giggle more as she headed up the stairs to her room. There was part of her that wanted to rebel and head out again, but a slight sway made her pause. Pouting, she decided that it would probably be best for her to actually rest for the night. Plus, she had been permitted to watch all the Space Buddies movies, an opportunity that she couldn't miss out on in the slightest.

She skipped the rest of the way to her room, distantly hearing the front door opening and then slamming shut. She grinned to herself, figuring that Alvin's newest boyfriend was already on the dump pile. Shaking her head, she opened her door and was deliberating over whether to take a shower or not when she spotted an intruder on her bed.

He was large, a deep shade of brown with a large white patch covering most of his face, big droopy ears and an eye-patch that had a silver monogram of a paw on it. Dressed in a dark blue space suit, with the company logo on the pocket and a pair of sturdy black boots, it was clear that he was someone very special indeed.

"CANINE PUP!" Sehseh squealed, suddenly launching her-self forward to grab the toy and pull it to her chest tightly, before spinning around in a happy circle. When Rhain got up-stairs two minutes later, Sehseh was still dancing around hap-pily, spinning and pirouetting whilst alternatively raising the toy high and then hugging it back to her chest. She stopped to smile brightly and say to it, "Finally I have you in my arms, where you belong, and you'll always be safe."

Rhain smiled too and tried desperately tried not to be spotted as he took photographs of this situation that was too adorable for words. Alvin chuckled from behind him, leaning on the wall. "Why you don't just tell her always baffles me."

"Because this brings her joy and some comfort," Rhain replied. "It takes time for her to collect them and-"

"THANK YOU!" Sehseh squealed, launching a glomp onto Rhain who only just managed to stop himself from falling over onto his face. "Thank you, thank you, thank you!"

Alvin fell over laughing and Rhain collapsed to the floor with Sehseh still squealing on top of him. It was nice to have something to laugh about, even if it was just their rather crazy Maid going hyper over a plush toy.

6

IN UNDERLAND

"What's the matter with you, Miya?" Mr Wirth asked the girl sitting at the window, watching the rain fall with no apparent enthusiasm for doing so.

Mr. Wirth was a tall man, athletically built with sharp features and hardened grey eyes. His hair was turning more steadily grey with the years but it was long and thin and woven into high buns so he still somehow managed to look young. He wore a grey suit, tailored to perfection and had a black watch PDA strapped to his wrist. Sensible shoes and a black scarf made him look almost regal and he carried a bag marked with FPStore in his left hand.

The constant blip of the red light on his left temple alerted the world to the fact that some part of him was working on other matters, perhaps the outcome of a deal he was engaged in. However, he still seemed alert and focused on the girl in front of him. Upon receiving the notification that his top assassin was back at base, the man thought it best to check on her. Hopefully, if things had gone to plan, his little plot would begin to take steps in the right direction.

Miya took a second or two to answer his question, before turning towards the man with a hurt expression, "She saw me."

"And?" Mr Wirth asked in return.

"She didn't recognise me," Miya replied, turning away. "She actually forgot me."

A smirk crossed Mr Wirth's face before it was replaced by a sympathetic smile. "People change, Miya. Maids are fickle in their emotions because they're all fake. Made up of code and numbers that can be altered if one knows how to do so." He walked around to stand next to Miya. "You should take it as a good thing that she doesn't remember you. It'll make things easier."

"But she made me a promise, Daddy," Miya replied, "and she broke it."

"Promises are made to be broken," the man replied, sitting down next to her. Lightly he stroked her long blonde hair. "But don't worry. No adult or infectious little Maid will ever hurt you again. I've helped you to grow into one of the most power-ful, accurate and amazing assassins in the world and soon the world will respect you and acknowledge your presence with-out even questioning their love for you."

The girl blinked and then smiled. "That's good to know. I look forward to that day."

"Here, I got you this for doing so well," Mr Wirth replied, handing the girl a box. "I'm sure it'll cheer you up."

The girl smiled and opened the box, her eyes going wide in surprise as she found inside a Canine Pup plush which she immediately hugged to her chest. "Thank you!" she grinned so brightly. "Thank you so much, Daddy! I shall take good care of him always."

Mr Wirth smiled as he watched the girl play with the toy, though it did not show in his eyes. How badly he wanted to chuckle then, knowing that soon these moments wouldn't even matter. The balance of power was almost tipping over to his favour and once that appalling excuse for a Maid was eliminated then everything else would fall into place.

He couldn't wait to see the other's face when she realised that she was going to be taken out by the girl she was sworn to protect. The one she could never harm or hurt, no matter what reprogramming they did to her.

TWICE
mini
F. P.

Tsuzuku

To Be Continued

CREATIVE TEAM

This Volume brought to you by

Sarah Elliot - Author - when not writing running around the woods, teaching kids all about them and desperately trying to avoid her artist who wants to stuff a paintbrush up her nose for not fully describing what a 'tight fitting top means' and for drawing chibis (something she hates)

Katrina Allcroft - Artist - chasing down the author to get more details of what on earth she means description wise whilst also finding many little cute references to slip into her art and coming up with more diabloical plans to throw art at author for volume 3

Boo Lai - Editor - pulled out of one workaholic box, sat down with some hot chocolate, giving editing stuff and being hugged and pampered whilst looking for other work boxes to go back into

Kurt Dalton - Co-Creator - the one who still thinks he shouldn't be mentioned as he only helped with bits and pieces, even though there were more than enough times that author had to message going 'how the hell do I get this to work!'